If You Want
To Be A Cat

First published in Great Britain in 1997 by
Macdonald Young Books
an imprint of Wayland Publishers Ltd
61 Western Road
Hove
East Sussex
BN3 1JD

Text copyright © Joyce Dunbar 1997
Illustrations copyright © Allan Curless 1997

Designed by Miriam Yarrien
Printed and bound in Belgium by Proost International Book Co.

British Library Cataloguing in Publication Data available.

ISBN: 0 7500 2438 0

JOYCE DUNBAR
IF YOU WANT TO BE A CAT

Illustrated by Allan Curless

MACDONALD YOUNG BOOKS

Rat-a-tat-tat!
Ten cats prick up their ears.
They open their eyes wide.
What's that?

A box with flaps.
A box with holes.
It shuffles.
It snuffles.

Then over . . .

. . . it rolls!

Then on to their chair, with one great bound,
A thingy, a whatsit, a jumblyboo.

The cats, so curious,
gather round,
And ask, politely,
"What are *you*?"

The whatsit answers,
"I wish I knew."

"Well," say the cats,
"Whether you're a whatsit, or a jumblyboo,
If you want to live here, you must do as cats do!"

"Watch it, whatsit, while we do our cat thing,

With a wriggly, windy, ball of string!"

"Hopeless! If you want to be a cat,
You must do it like this, not that!"

"Walkies, whatsit, along the railings,
Then lightly across these painted palings."

"Clumsy! If you want to be a cat,
You must do it like this, not that!"

CA

T S ! ود

It was a glorious game, wonderful fun,
But all too soon, it was over and done.
Now here's a puzzle, where *is* everyone?

The whatsit waits awhile
under a tree.
Where have they gone?
Where can they be?
Alone he sits, all, all alone,
At last he makes his weary way home.

Not there, not here, not anywhere.
"Oh well," sighs the whatsit,
"I don't care,
For I'm not a cat,
I don't do it like that, but . . .

. . . like this!"

And the whatsit slumps in a heap for a nap,
While flip goes the cat-flap, flap-flip-flap,
And the cats, so curious, gather round,
To see their whatsit safe and sound,
And oh so cosy, just so snug,
Now they know what he is.
He's a shaggy, doggy . . .

. . . RUG!